Minnie's Tea Party

Minnie Mouse and her best friend
Daisy Duck looked through
the ruffled curtains on
Minnie's bedroom window. The
sky was dark and it was pouring rain.

"I guess we can't go outside," Minnie sighed.

"Then what will we do all day?" Daisy asked. "Can you think
of anything?"

The two friends looked around Minnie's pretty pink and
white room with its dolls, stuffed animals, and little pink table.

"I know," Minnie exclaimed. "Let's have a tea party! We'll dress up and pretend we're princesses in an enchanted castle. There's a trunk full of old clothes in the attic. C'mon! Follow me!"

"This is going to be fun!" Daisy said, excitedly, as they moved stacks and stacks of dusty boxes out of the way.

"Look, here it is!" cried Minnie when they had found the trunk. The girls threw open the lid and looked inside.

"Wow, we'll look like royalty in these," Daisy said as she held up a flowered skirt and a scarf with lots of beads.

Daisy put on a pair of high heel slippers with pom poms on the toes and imagined herself bowing to a handsome prince. Minnie chose a long purple gown and a floaty pink scarf.

"Look Daisy," she said, putting on a pair of green high heels. "These are my emerald slippers."

Minnie could just see herself dancing in a castle ballroom. She and Daisy gazed at themselves in Minnie's mirror, and there were two princesses smiling right back.

"Wait! Princesses have crowns!" said Daisy. "And jewels, and things like that."

"I know!" said Minnie. "I saved a bunch of stones from some old jewelry I had. Let's make crowns and decorate them. Then we'll look like real princesses."

Daisy and Minnie got out crayons, and scissors, and paper. First they cut out crowns. Then they cut out necklaces and bracelets. After they had colored them gold and silver, Minnie got out her jewelry box. Daisy and Minnie stuck down as many beautiful jewels as they could fit on their paper cutouts.

"Don't we look beautiful?" said Minnie, looking in the mirror.

"Of course. Princesses always look beautiful," said Daisy.

Next Minnie and Daisy set the table. Daisy draped a sheet over it then added some ribbon and homemade paper roses. Next Minnie gathered some flowers from an old straw hat and put them in the middle of the table. "Here is a beautiful bouquet from our royal garden," she told Daisy.

They both giggled. Minnie found her tea set in the toy chest. "It's only plastic," she said, "but we can pretend it's pure gold and covered with diamonds and rubies!"

"Emeralds, too!" added Daisy.

"Now let's go to the royal kitchen and prepare the royal tea!" said Minnie.

In a few minutes, they had poured apple juice into the teapot and prepared a tray with peanut butter crackers and chocolate cookies.

"Aren't these fancy cakes the Royal Baker made just divine?" Minnie said.

"Oh, yes," Daisy agreed. "He's outdone himself this time. Just look at all that whipped cream!"

Now, it was time to invite the guests.

"Princess Daisy and Princess Minnie request the honor of your presence at a royal tea party," they told Minnie's favorite teddy bear, Mr. Bear.

"Thank you," Minnie made Mr. Bear growl back.

"Please do come," Daisy bowed to the dolls.

"We'd be delighted," Minnie made the dolls seem to answer.

Then, one by one, all the dolls and stuffed animals sat around the fancy table.

The two princesses and their

subjects nibbled on royal

treats and gossiped about life around

the kingdom. When they were finished, Minnie's bedroom

was bathed in sunlight.

"Look Minnie! We were having so much fun, we forgot all

about the rain," Daisy said.

"Indeed we did, Princess Daisy," Minnie answered. "In

fact, I think we should have a royal tea at the castle every

time it rains!"

Daisy and Minnie took off their costumes and went outside into the bright sunshine. "Should we take a stroll through the royal garden?" Minnie asked.

"Why, yes," replied Daisy. "I hear there's an afternoon tea being held in the gazebo."

"Another tea party! Oh, Dear! I'm afraid I couldn't eat another thing!" exclaimed Minnie.

Then the princesses laughed, and began to plan what they would pretend to be tomorrow.